YET ANOTHER GOOD REASON
TO BE AFRAID OF THE DARK.

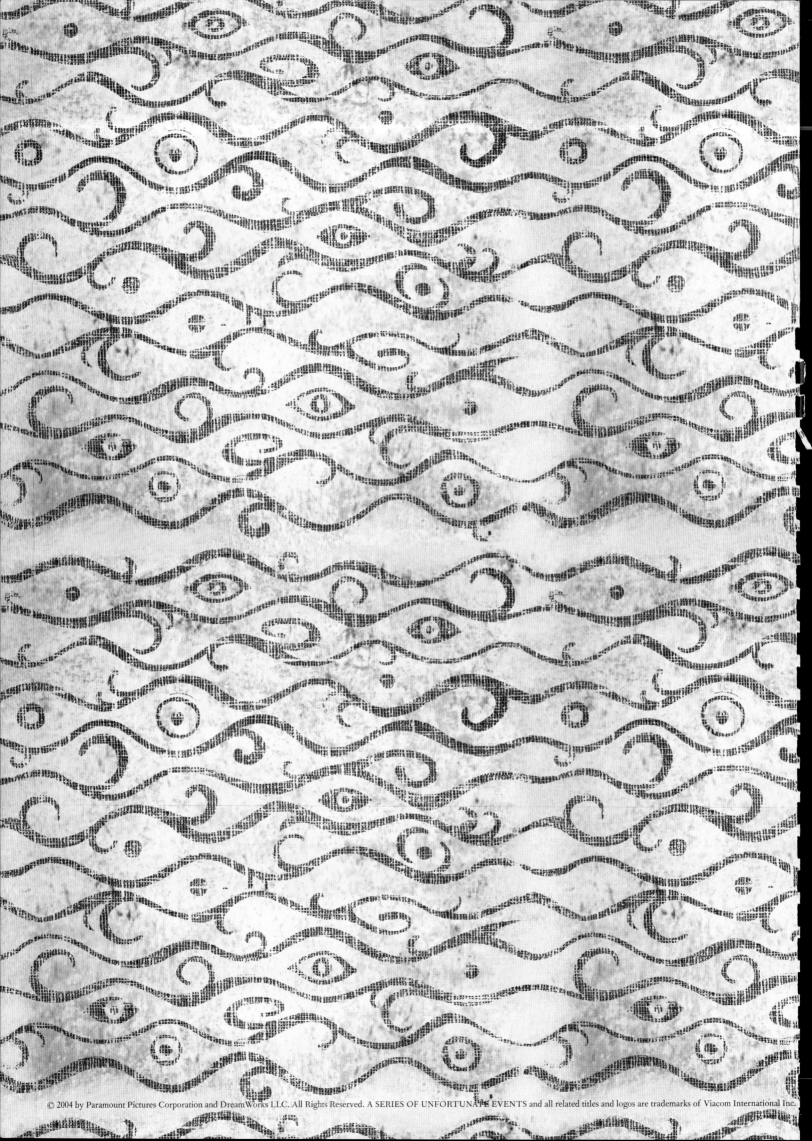

THERE IS NOTHING MORE PLEASANT THAN ARRIVING HOME,
UNLESS IT IS THE HOME OF SOMEONE UNPLEASANT.

THIS MAN IS COMPLETELY CROOKED.

JAILBIRDS OF A FEATHER PLOT TOGETHER.

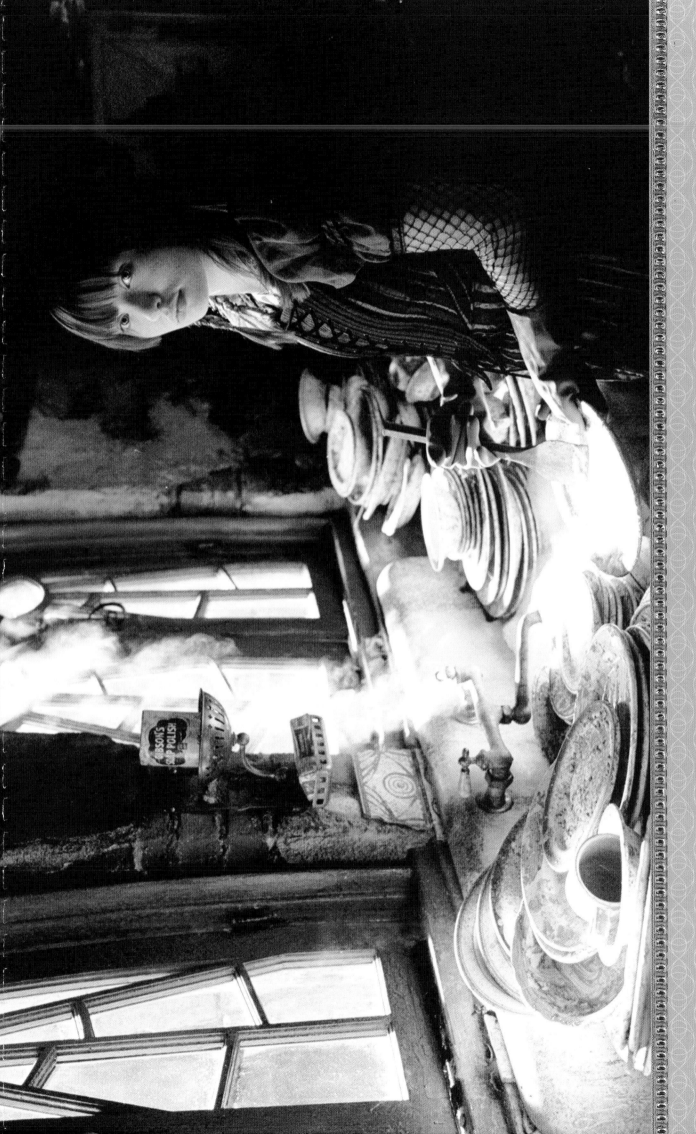

THERE IS NOTHING MORE DISGUSTING THAN A PLATE RECENTLY LICKED BY SOMEONE DISGUSTING.

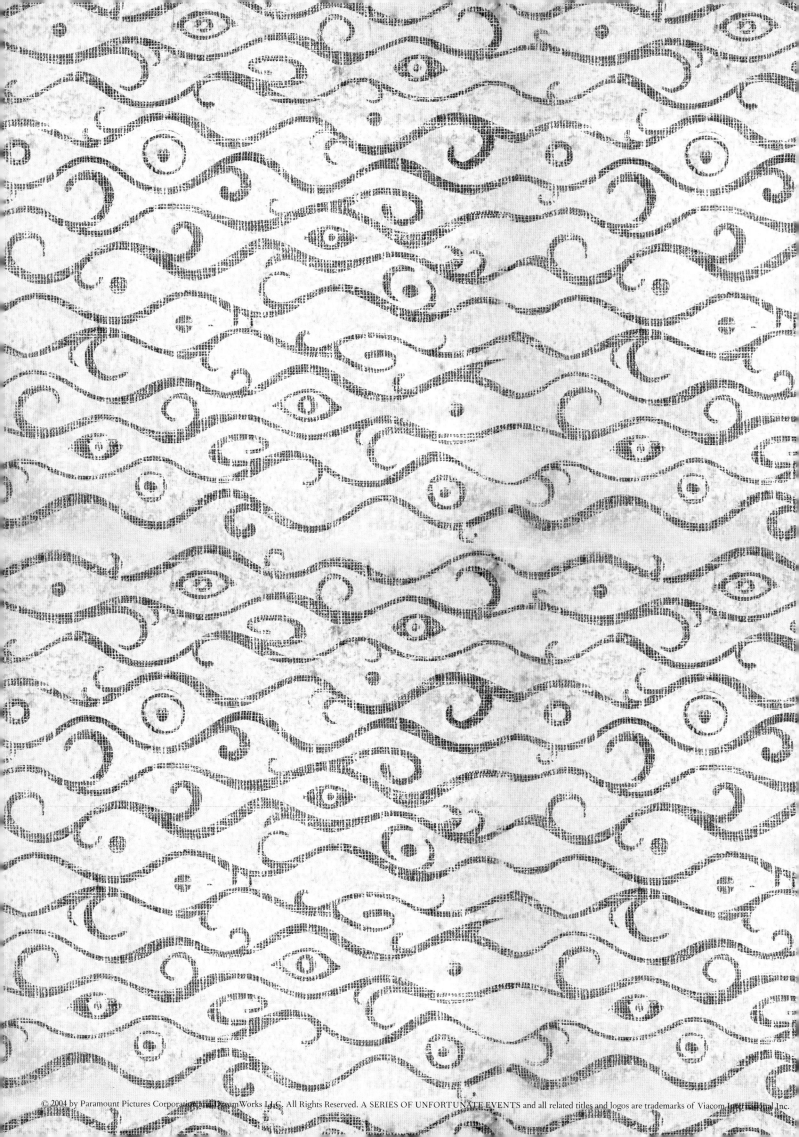

CAUTION: CERTAIN CHORES MAY BE DANGEROUS, POISONOUS, FATAL, OR ALL THREE.

THERE ARE MANY DIFFERENT VARIETIES OF SNAKE.
THIS IS ONE OF THE MOST DANGEROUS.

IT IS GRAMMATICALLY INCORRECT FOR A PERSON
TO RUN SCREAMINGLY FOR HER LIFE,
BUT THAT DOESN'T MEAN IT DOESN'T HAPPEN.

NOW WOULD BE A GOOD TIME
TO PUT ON A LIFE JACKET.

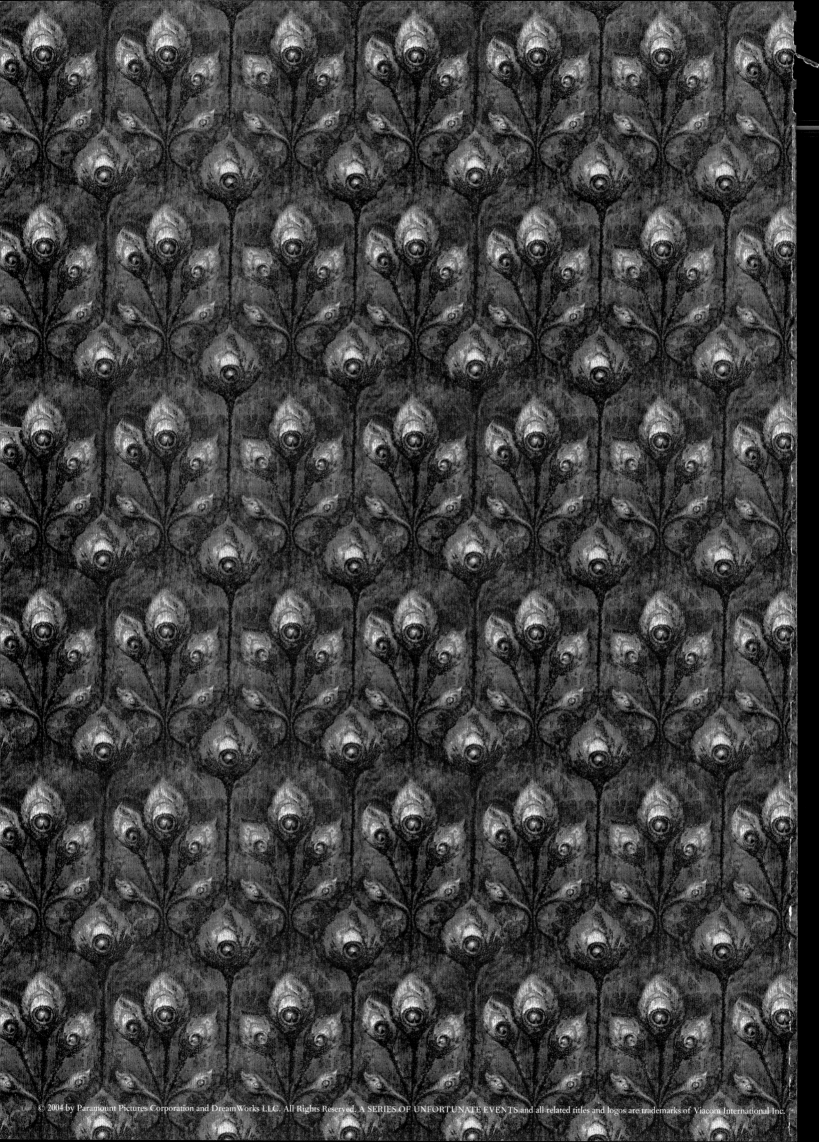

NEVER LOOK A GIFT HORSE IN THE MOUTH.
IT MIGHT BE SOMEONE YOU KNOW.

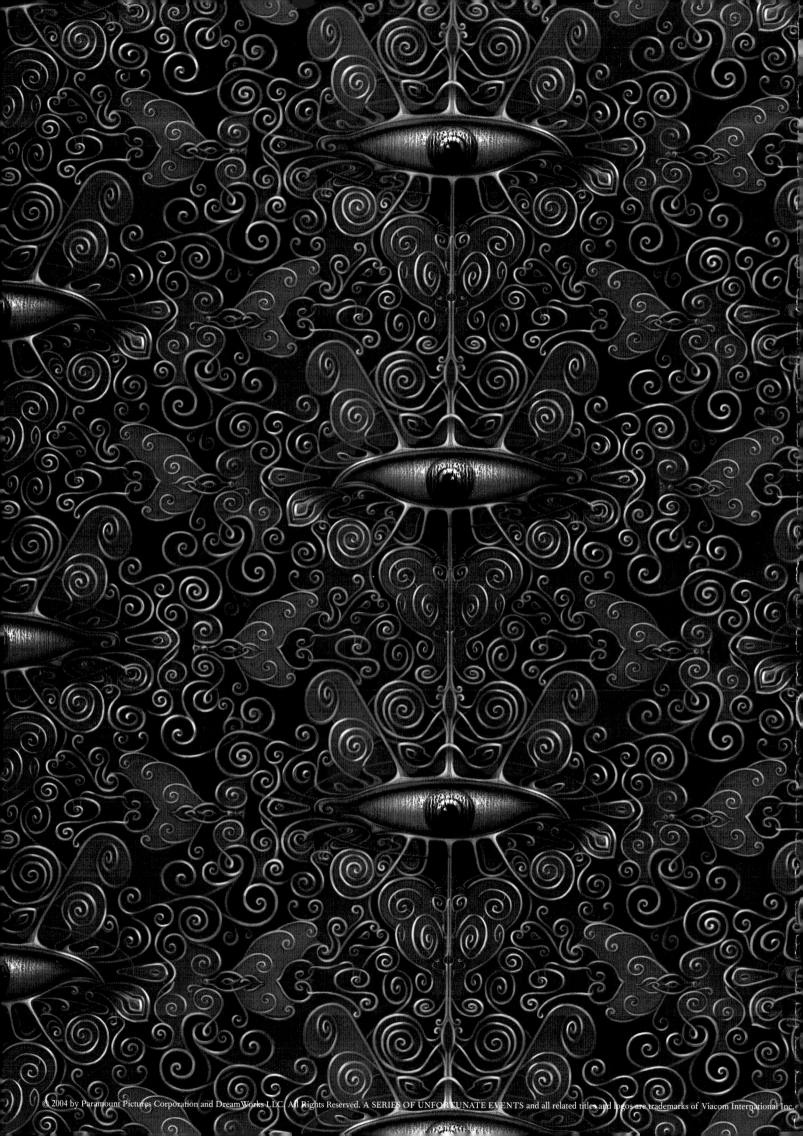

DON'T TRY THIS AT HOME,
UNLESS SOMEBODY HAS IMPRISONED YOUR BABY SISTER
IN A CAGE HUNG FROM THE TOP OF A HIGH TOWER.

IT IS DIFFICULT TO ESCAPE THE TRUTH,
UNLESS YOU ARE ATTACHED TO STURDY WIRE
DESIGNED FOR THAT PURPOSE.

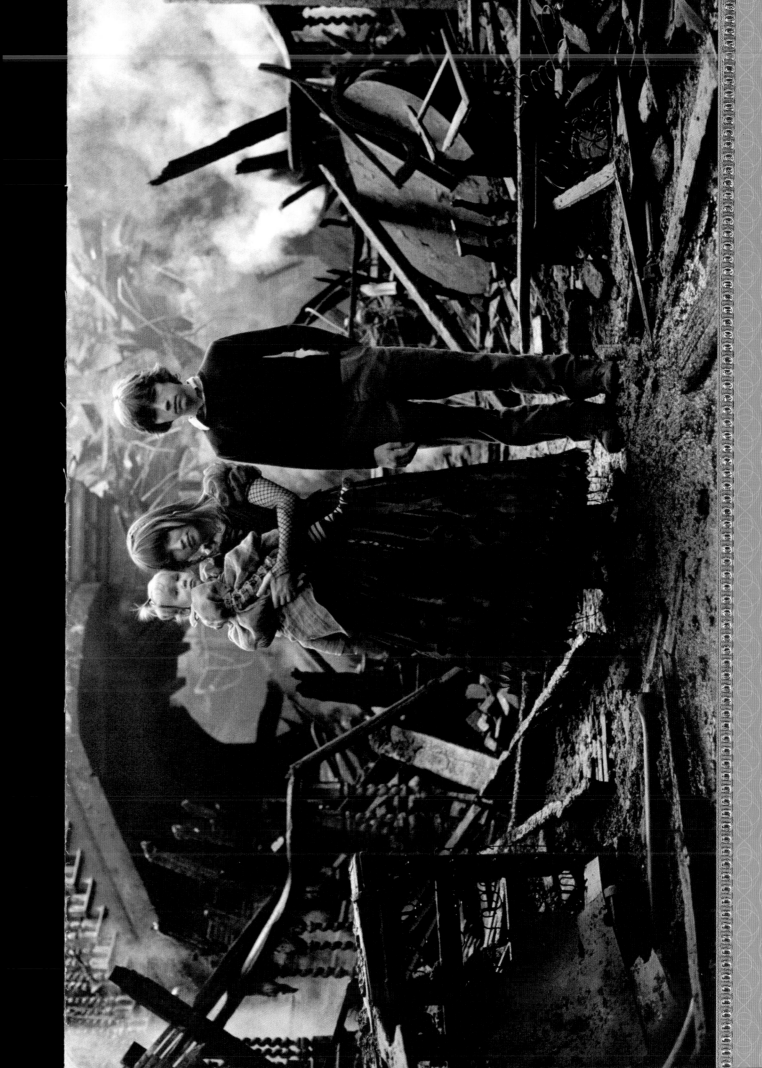

A STORY THAT BEGINS WITH FIRE OUGHT TO END IMMEDIATELY.

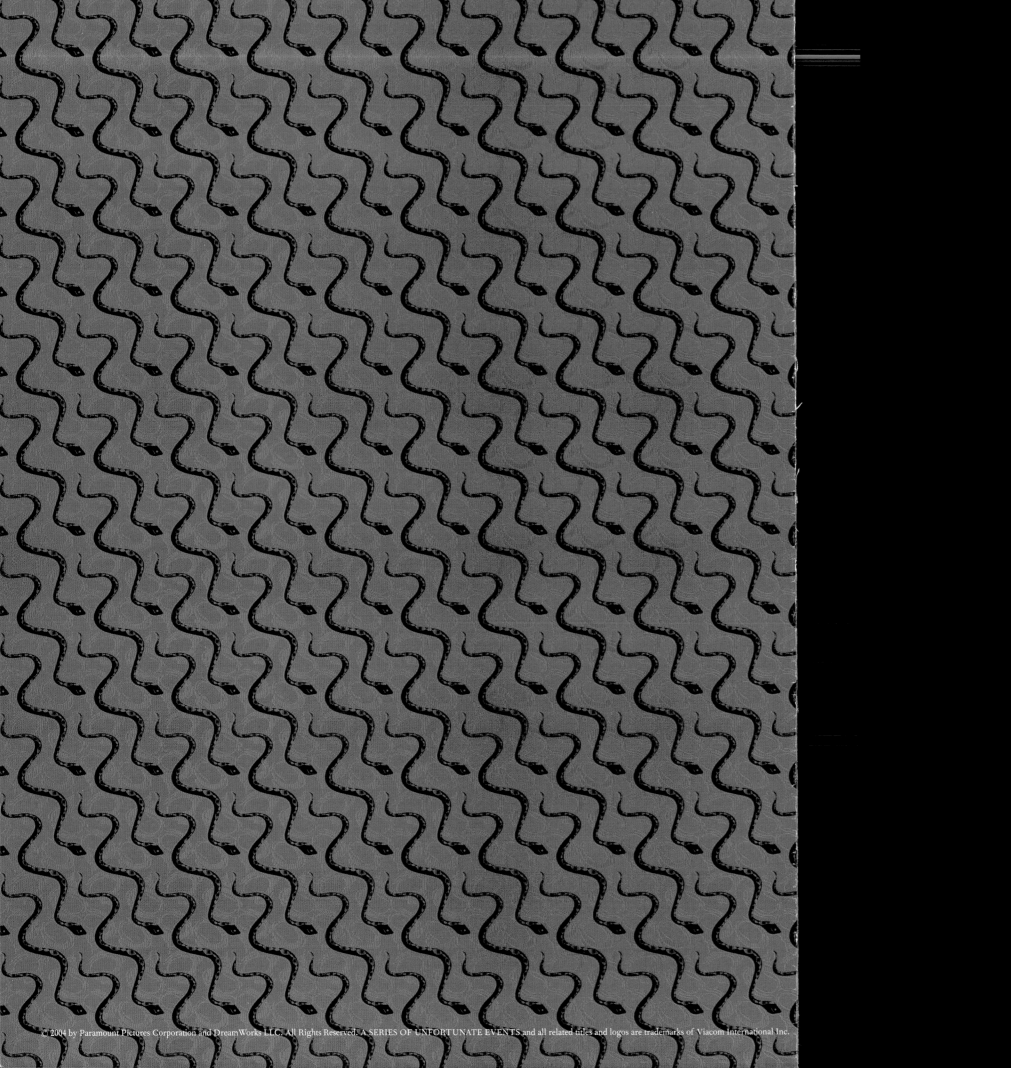